A Good Fish Dinner

A GOOD FISH DINNER

by Barbara K. Walker
pictures by Art Cumings

Parents' Magazine Press • *New York*

Dedicated, with love, to three little foxes,
The Newman girls, Tracy, Vicki, Carol

Text copyright © 1978 by Barbara K. Walker
Illustrations copyright © 1978 by Art Cumings
All rights reserved
Printed in the United States of America
10 9 8 7 6 5 4 3 2 1

Library of Congress Cataloging in Publication Data

Walker, Barbara K. A good fish dinner.

SUMMARY: A fox steals a fine dinner from a
fish-seller, but a wolf, following his example,
is not so lucky.
[1. Foxes—Fiction. 2. Wolves—Fiction]
I. Cumings, Art. II. Title.
PZ7.W15215Go 1979   [E]   78-11152
ISBN 0-08193-0983-4   ISBN 0-8193-0984-2 lib. bdg.

ne day a fox said to himself,
"I'm hungry!
But what can I find to eat?"

He sniffed. He looked. He listened.
Suddenly, he heard a rumbling noise.

Along came a fish-seller driving to market.
On his cart was a fine load of fish.
"Aha!" said the fox. *"Fish* for dinner."

He had a plan. He ran as fast
as he could through the woods.

"Here's the road again.
I'll lie in the dust and play dead," said he.

Then, in a little while, along came the
fish-seller, driving his cart to market.
"Aha! A dead fox!" he said.

"I'll just take him along with me.
His fine fur will fetch a good price."
He jumped down from his cart.

He picked up the fox by one leg.
He shook him and shook him.
"There! The dust is gone from your coat."

"Now, up you go!" said he.
And he tossed the fox
on top of his load of fish.
The fish-seller climbed back
onto his cart and drove off.

"There's a one, and a two, and a three."
The fox was counting,
no more dead than you or I.

And each time he counted,
he threw another fish off the cart.
"There are three fat fish for my dinner.
What a fine meal for a fox!"
He leaped down from the cart.

He ran back along the road.
"Here's a one, and a two, and a three,"
he said. And he picked up the fine fat fish.

Then, he ran.
"I'll eat my dinner in the woods," said he.

"Mm-m-m!"
He licked the last of the bones.
He looked up.

There sat the wolf.

"How did you catch those fish, Friend Fox?
I'd like some fish myself!"

"It's very easy, Friend Wolf," said the fox.

"I fished on the fish-seller's cart.
You can fish there, too.
But, mind you, count softly," he said.

"Of course!" said the wolf.
And away he ran.

"Here's a place well ahead on the road.
I'll lie in the dust, dead as dead," said he.
Then, along came the fish-seller,
driving his cart to market.

"Aha! A dead wolf!" he said.
"This is my lucky day.
I'll just take him along with me.
His fine fur will fetch a good price."
He jumped down from his cart.

He picked up the wolf by one leg.
He shook and he shook him.
"There! The dust is gone from your coat."

"Now, up you go!" said he.
And he tossed the wolf
on top of his load of fish.
The fish-seller climbed back
onto his cart and drove off.

"There's a one, and a two, and a three."
The wolf was counting,
no more dead than you or I.

And each time he counted,
he threw another fish off the cart.
"Why should I stop at three?" said he.
"There's a four, and a five, and a six!"
He laughed out loud as he counted.
"You stopped too soon, Friend Fox!"

The fish-seller heard him. "What's this!"
he cried. And he turned around to see.

The fox was gone, but the wolf
was still counting.
"And a seven, and an eight, and a nine!"

"So you stole my fox and my fish,
you rascal!"

The fish-seller picked up his stick,
and gave the wolf a hard whack.
And the wolf fell, dead as dead.

"Away to the market we'll go:
that greedy gray wolf,
and the rest of my fish,
and I and my cart!" he said.

About the Author

Barbara K. Walker, author of such popular Parents' books as *The Dancing Palm Tree; New Patches For Old* and *The Round Sultan and the Straight Answer* did graduate work in folklore at Cornell University. A teacher of children's literature, storyteller, playwright and songwriter, Mrs. Walker lives in Lubbock, Texas, with her husband and two children.

About the Artist

Art Cumings, a graduate of Pratt Institute, has illustrated several children's books, including *Charlie's Pet* by Kate Ernst and Dr. Seuss's *The First of Octember.* His drawings have appeared in *Time, Saturday Review* and *Field and Stream* among other magazines. With *A Good Fish Dinner,* we welcome Mr. Cumings as an illustrator to Parents' Magazine Press's list. An avid jogger and tennis player, Art Cumings and his wife live in Douglaston, Long Island.